24 Hour Telephone Renewals 020 84

HARINGEY LIBRARIES

THIS BOOK MUST BE RETURNED

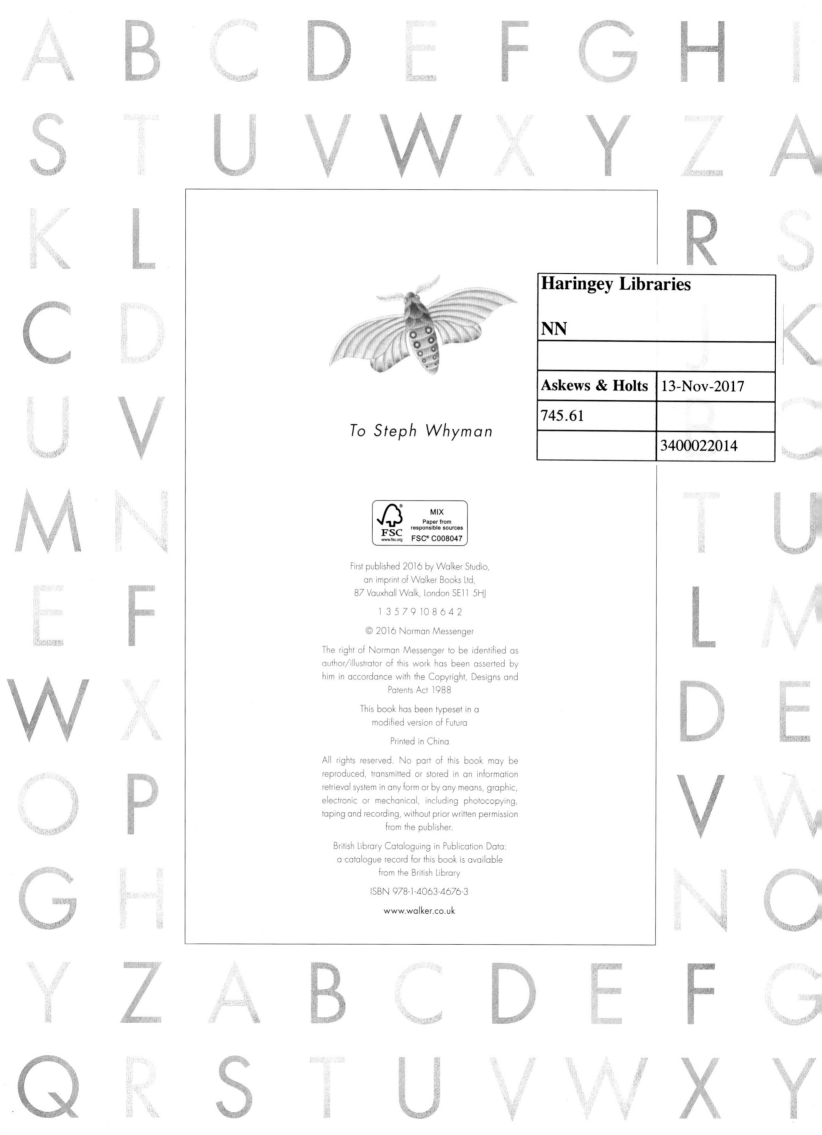

To Steph Whyman

MIX
Paper from
responsible sources
FSC
www.fsc.org   FSC® C008047

First published 2016 by Walker Studio,
an imprint of Walker Books Ltd,
87 Vauxhall Walk, London SE11 5HJ

1 3 5 7 9 10 8 6 4 2

© 2016 Norman Messenger

The right of Norman Messenger to be identified as
author/illustrator of this work has been asserted by
him in accordance with the Copyright, Designs and
Patents Act 1988

This book has been typeset in a
modified version of Futura

Printed in China

British Library Cataloguing in Publication Data:
a catalogue record for this book is available
from the British Library

ISBN 978-1-4063-4676-3

www.walker.co.uk

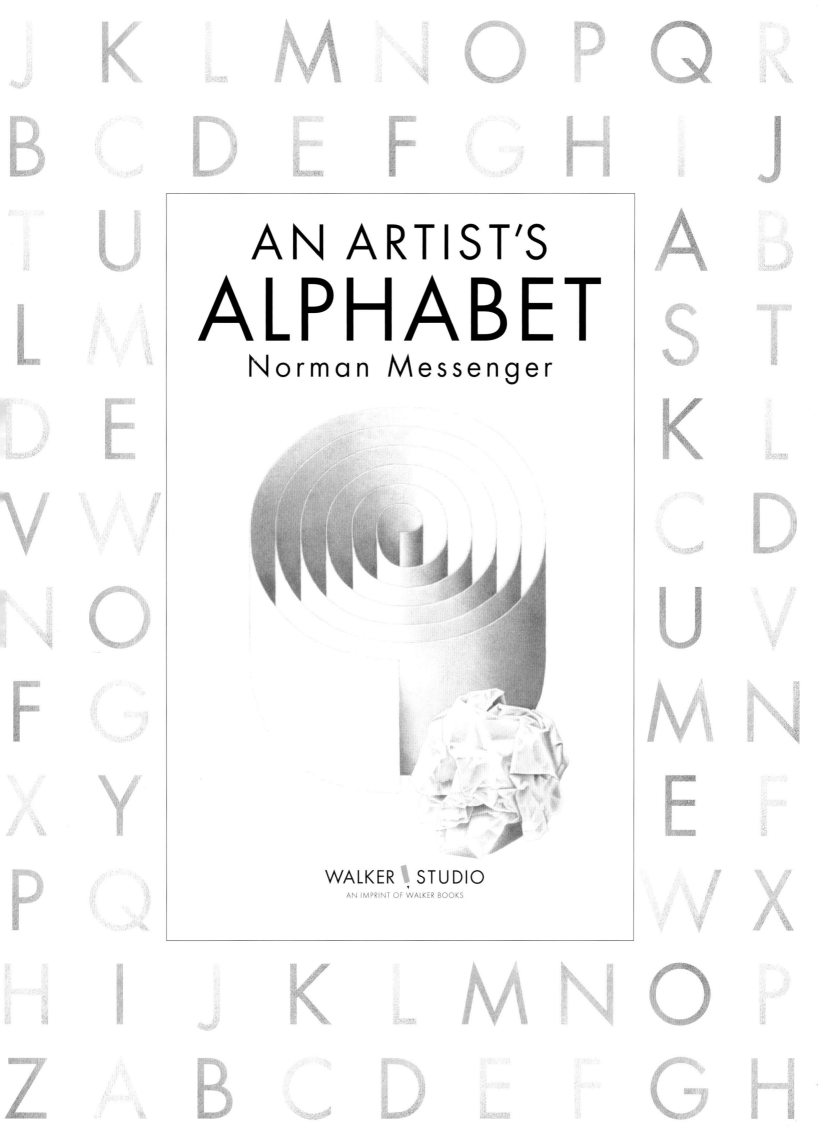

AN ARTIST'S
ALPHABET
Norman Messenger

WALKER STUDIO
AN IMPRINT OF WALKER BOOKS

Aa

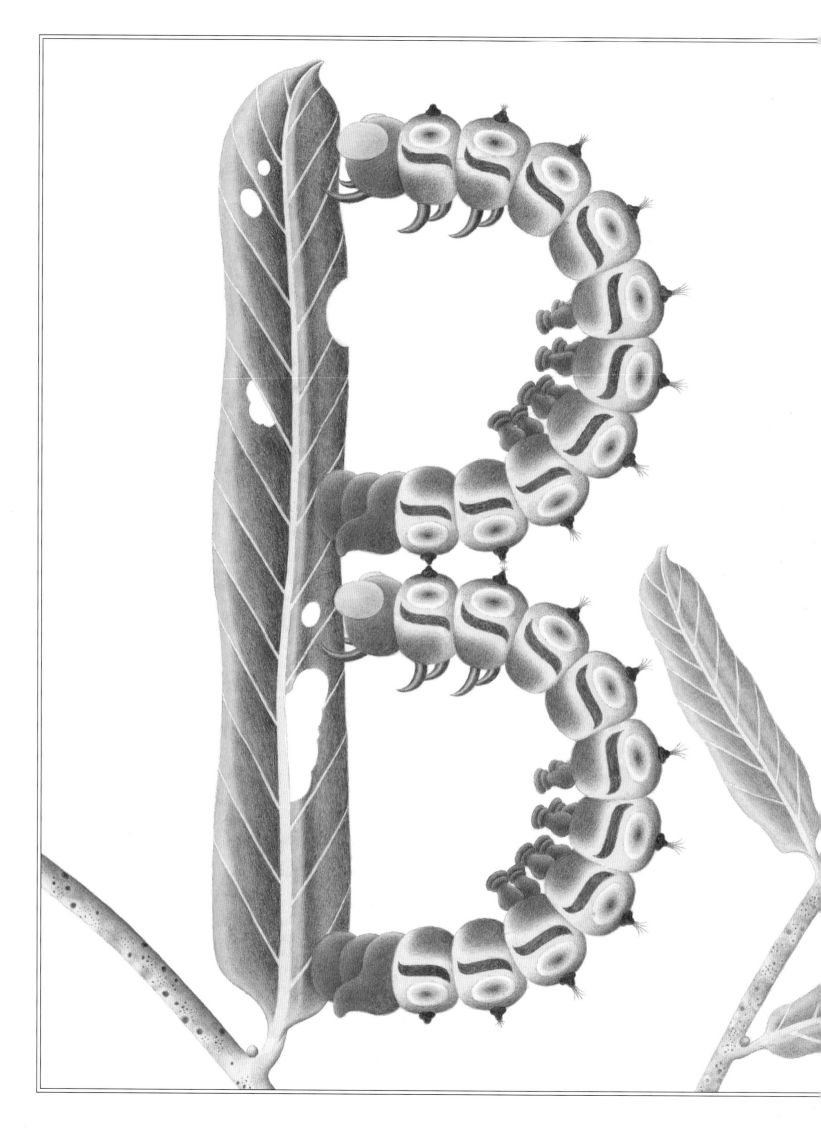

Bb

Cc

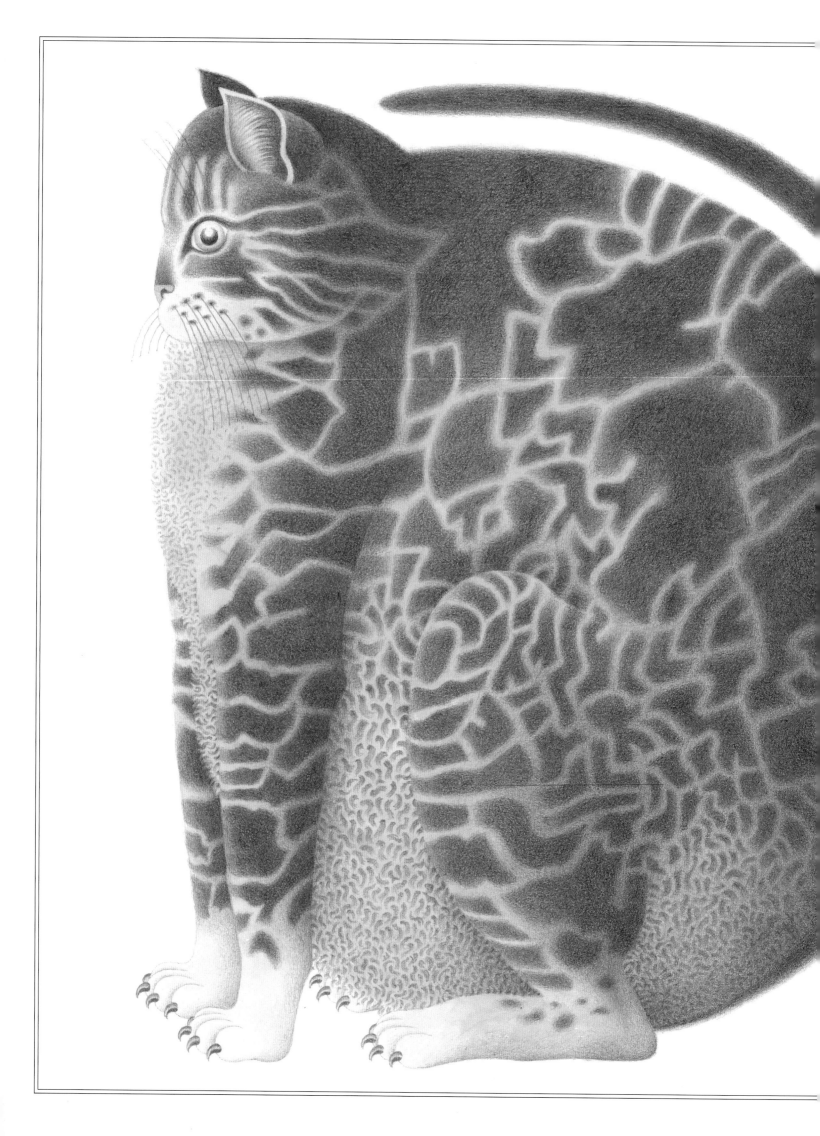

Dd

Ee

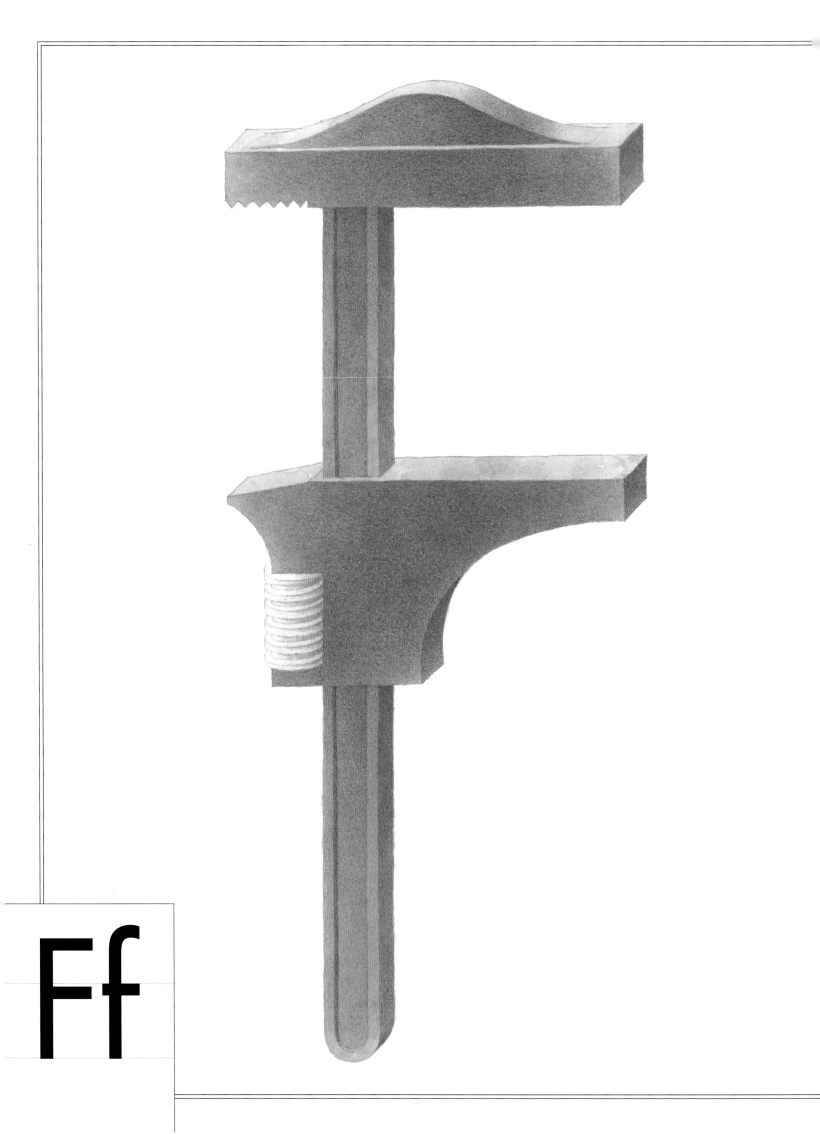

Ff

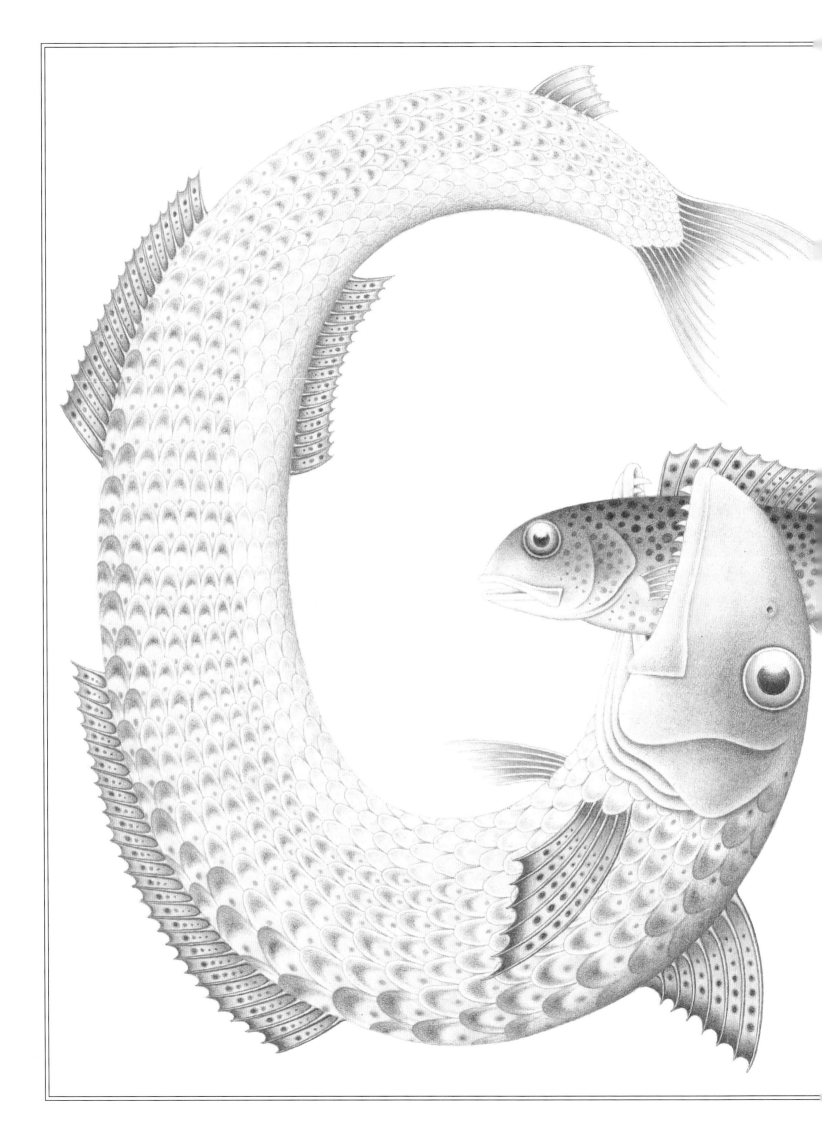

Gg

Hh

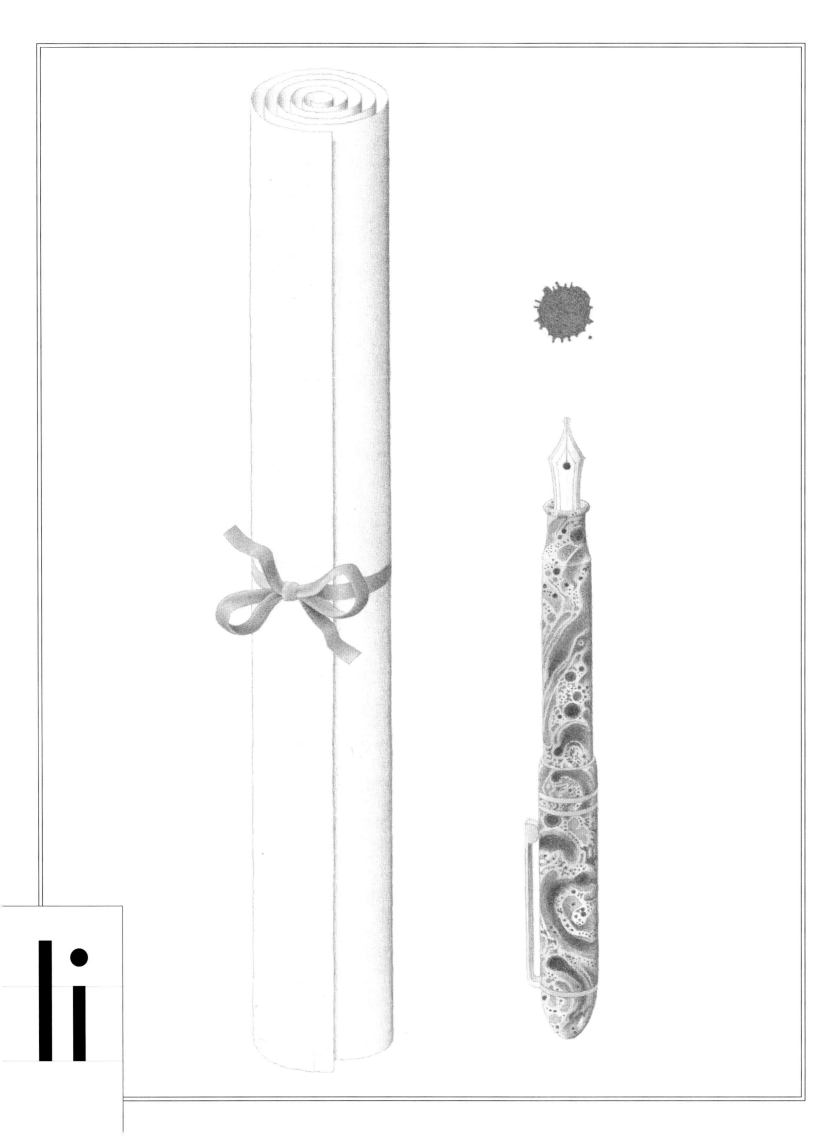

li

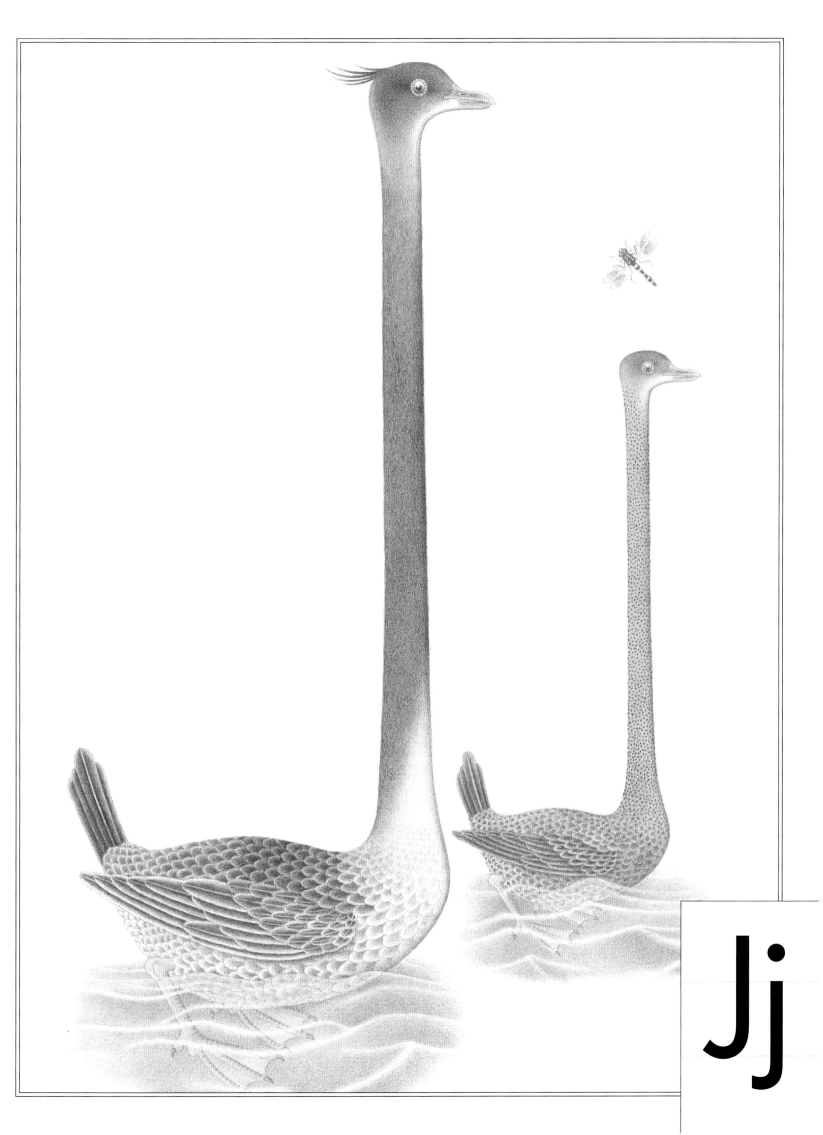

Jj

Kk

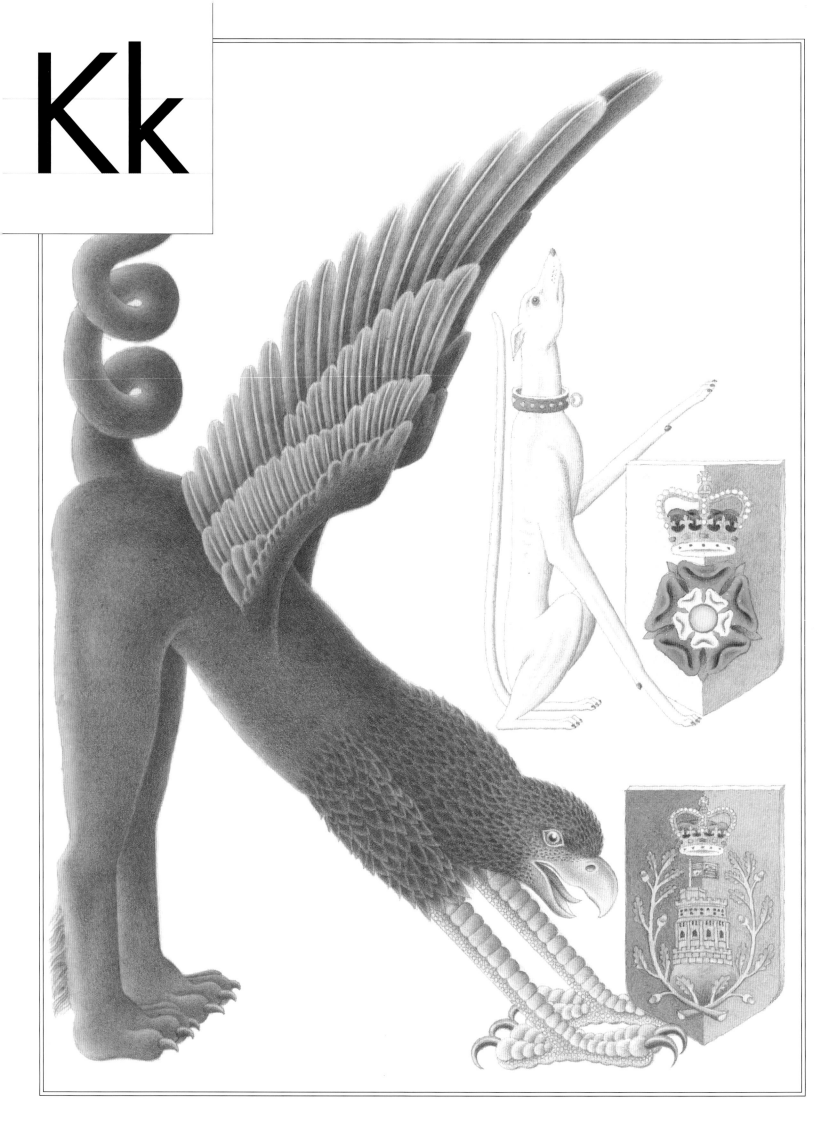

LI

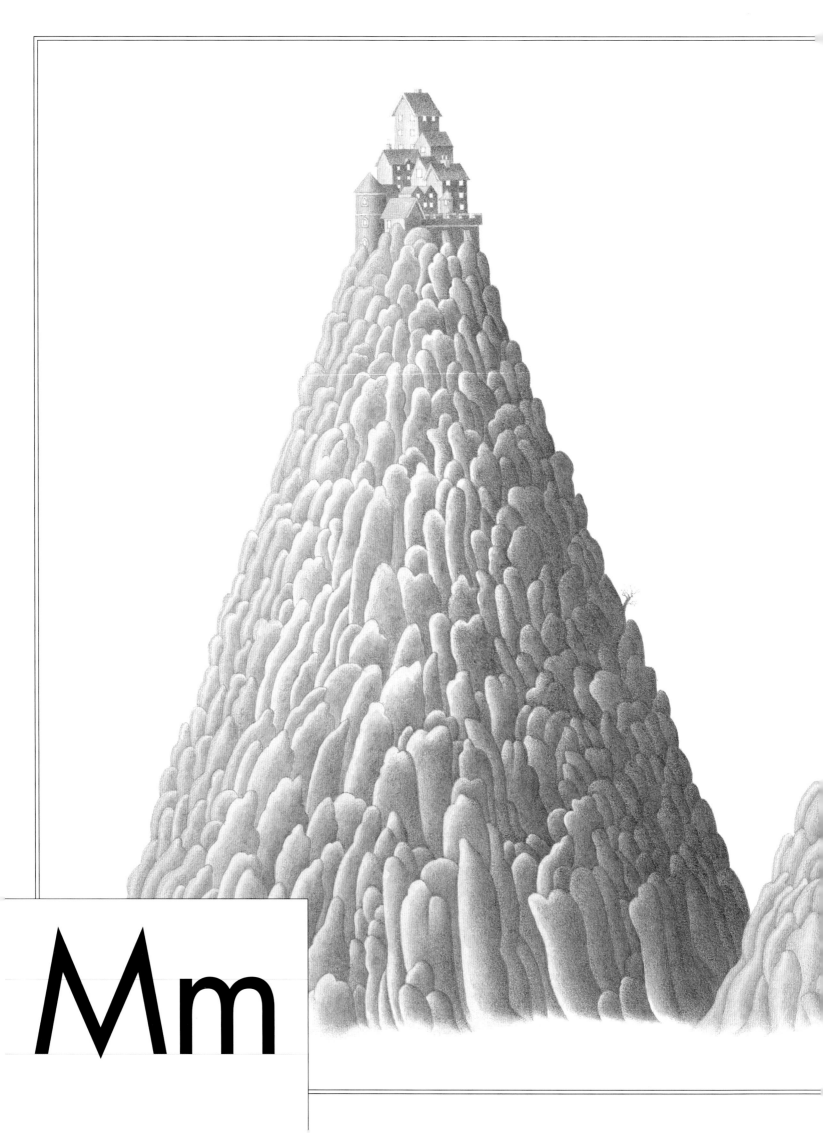

Mm

Nn

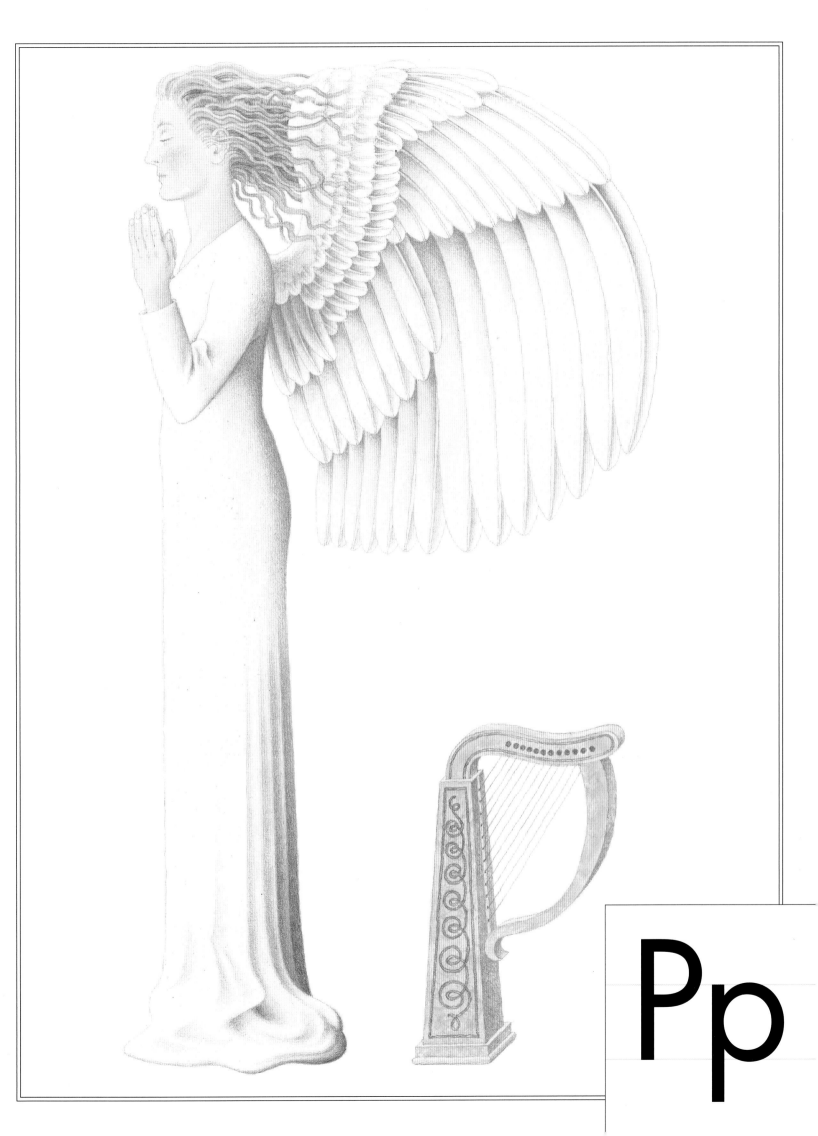

Pp

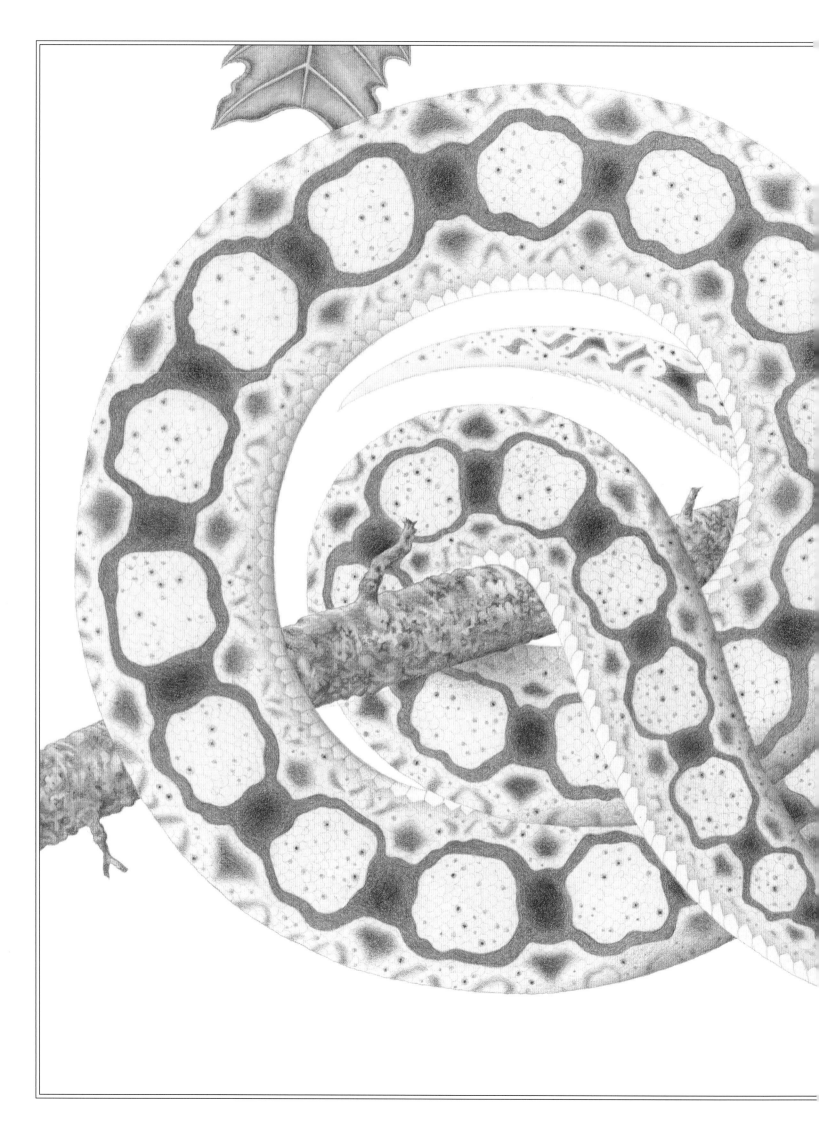

Qq

Rr

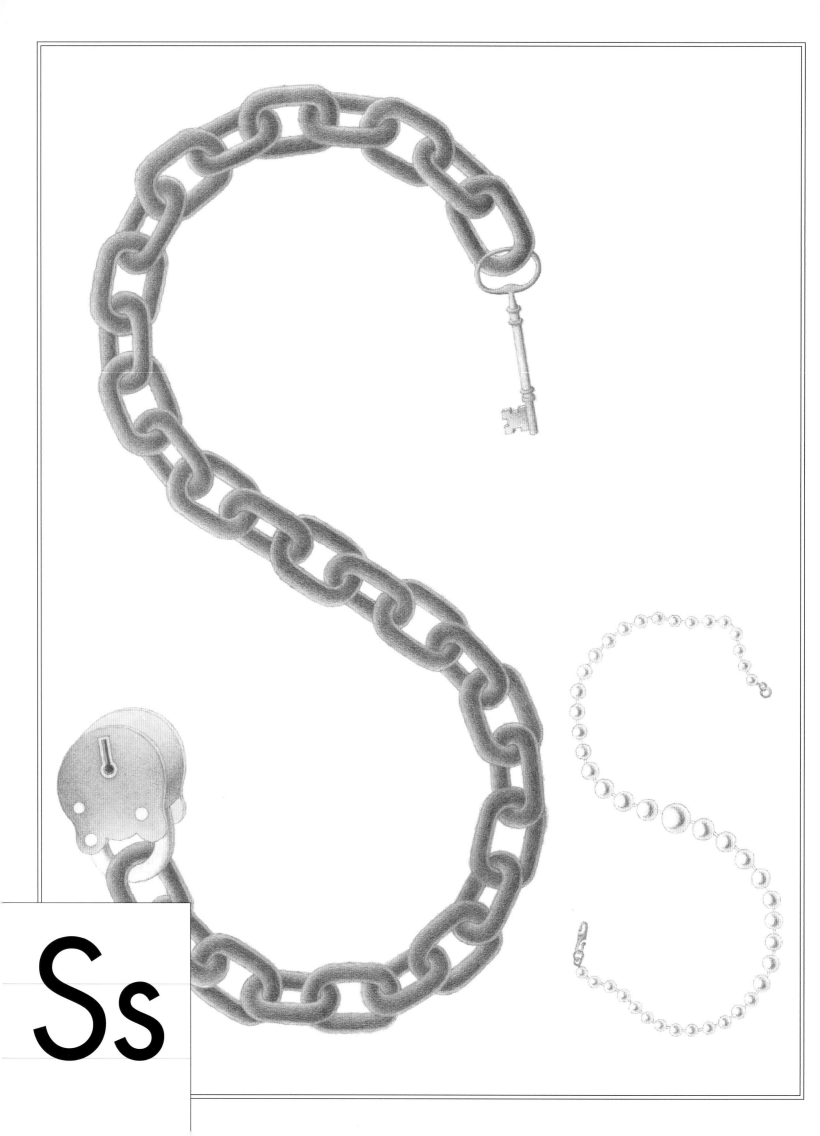

Ss

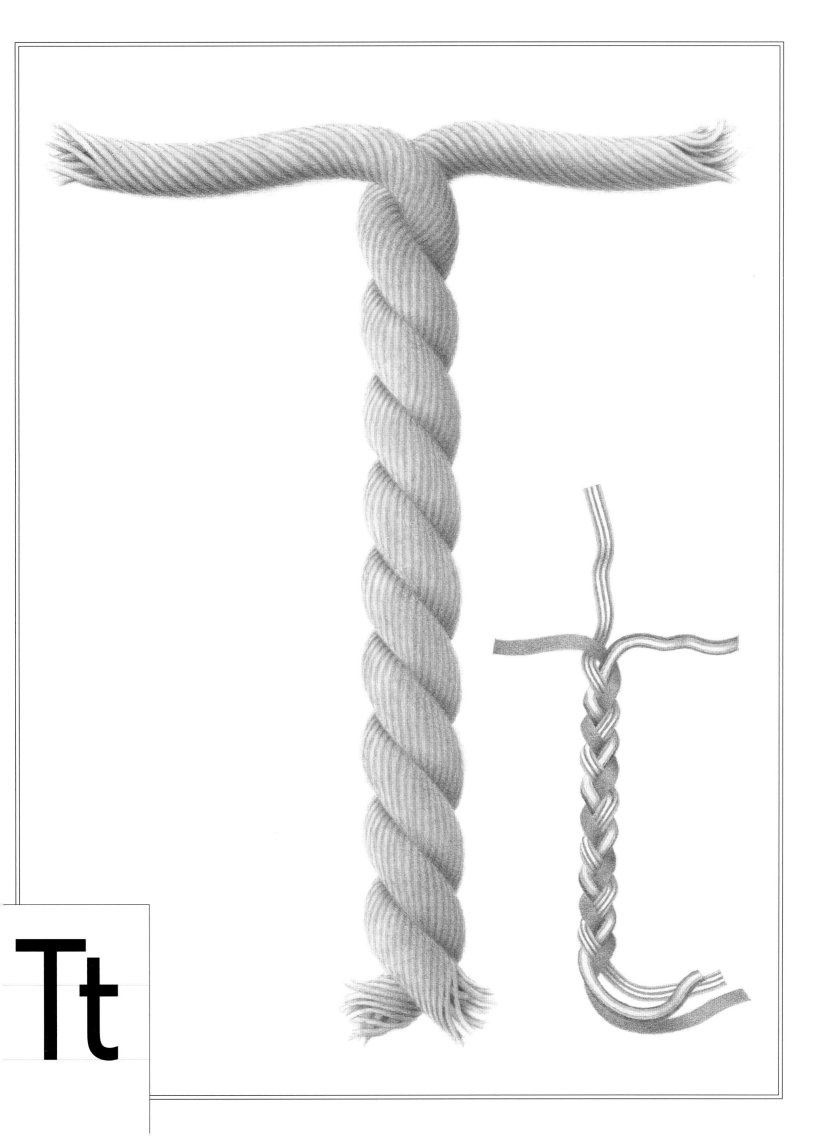

Tt

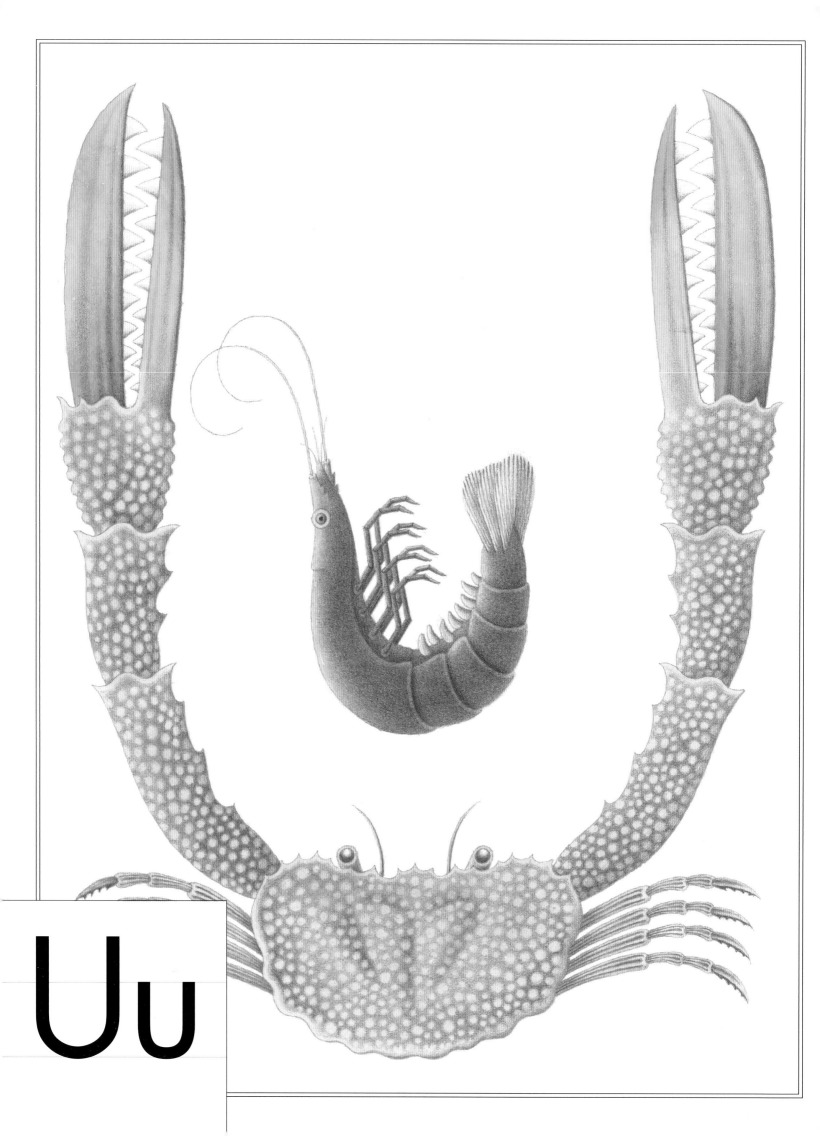

Uu

Vv

Ww

Xx

Yy

Zz